First published in 2017 by
Andersen Press Limited
20 Vauxhall Bridge Road
London SW1V 2SA
www.andersenpress.co.uk

2 4 6 8 10 9 7 5 3 1

British Library Cataloguing in Publication Data available.

ISBN 978 1 78344 529 5

Printed and bound in Great Britain by
Clays Limited, Bungay, Suffolk, NR35 1ED

The Dragonsitter Detective

Josh Lacey

Illustrated by Garry Parsons

Andersen Press
London

Welcome!

Sorry I can't be here to meet you, but I have been summoned to the port. They need my help preparing the submarine for hunting the Kraken.

Make yourselves at home.

Back soon.

Morton

PS I've left food in the cupboard for the dragons.

From: Edward Smith–Pickle

To: Morton Pickle

Date: Saturday 2 April

Subject: Scotland

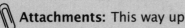 **Attachments:** This way up

Dear Uncle Morton

We've arrived!

Gordon picked us up from the train station and brought us to your island in his boat.

Thanks for leaving the note and the key.

Your dragons were very pleased to see us. I couldn't find their food in the cupboard, so I gave them some chocolate instead.

Ziggy had eleven Twixes, six Snickers and two boxes of Maltesers.

Arthur had nineteen mini Mars Bars.

They haven't been sick. Yet.

Mum says when will you be back?

1

She's worried you've forgotten about giving her away at the wedding, not to mention making a speech at the dinner afterwards.

She's in a bit of a panic because of the arrangements. Apparently getting married is very complicated, even if you've done it before.

I hope she cheers up before next Saturday, or she and Gordon aren't going to enjoy their own wedding.

Love from

Eddie

PS What's a kraken?

Dear Uncle Morton

Are you sitting down?

If you're not, you probably should, because I have some very bad news.

Someone has stolen one of your dragons.

This afternoon Ziggy was taken away by two thieves in a speedboat.

I don't know who they were. I couldn't see their faces properly.

I was on Lookout Point with Arthur, watching puffins through my binoculars, while Ziggy had a snooze on the beach.

Suddenly I heard a loud bang.

4

When I turned round, I saw a man with a gun. Ziggy was lying on the sand with a dart sticking out of her tummy.

A woman was tying a net around her.

I suppose the dart must have sent her to sleep, because the man and the woman dragged Ziggy along the beach, and she didn't even struggle.

I charged down the hill towards them.

Arthur flew ahead of me. He was desperate to help his mum.

We went as fast as we could, but we weren't fast enough. By the time we got down to the beach, it was too late. They had already loaded Ziggy into a speedboat.

The engines roared, then the boat turned round and cut through the waves, whizzing away from your island.

Arthur tried to follow his mum and rescue her, but as you know, he's still not very good at flying. He had only just got out to sea when he looped the loop in mid-air, then plummeted into the water.

I had to wade in and fetch him.

By that time the speedboat had completely disappeared.

I'm very sorry, Uncle Morton. We've only been in your house for a day, and already one of your dragons has been stolen.

Eddie

Dear Uncle Morton

Today Mr McDougall took me to the police station in Upper Buckett, where I reported Ziggy missing.

The policewoman said they don't have time to look for lost pets. She wasn't even interested in my pictures of the speedboat. She suggested I should do some detective work myself.

So I have.

I borrowed your magnifying glass. I hope you don't mind. I promise I'll be very careful.

I have been combing the beach for clues.

So far I have found
several interesting
footprints . . .

. . . and a small
green ticket
which says
ADMIT ONE.

Mum thinks it's probably a cinema ticket.

Gordon says the nearest cinema is twenty
miles away.

I want to go there and ask if they've seen
any dragons, but Mum says it's too far.

9

FIG 10. KRAKEN

I'm sure you're very busy with the Kraken. I looked it up in one of your books, and I can see how big it is.

I hope your submarine is big too, or the Kraken might wrap you in its enormous tentacles and drag you down to the bottom of the ocean.

But before you start searching for it, could you help me look for Ziggy? I don't think I can find her on my own.

Eddie

From: Edward Smith–Pickle

To: Morton Pickle

Date: Tuesday 5 April

Subject: Still missing

 Attachments: Bridesmaid

Dear Uncle Morton

Mum says, Where are you?

I said you've probably been held up by the Kraken, but Mum said a big squid is no reason to be late for your own sister's wedding.

I explained the Kraken isn't just any old big squid. It is actually the largest sea creature on the planet.

Mum said even so, you ought to be back by now.

I wish you would come home. I'm trying to find your dragon on my own, but I'm not a very good detective.

Mum won't help. She said she's run off her feet organising flowers for the church.

I said I didn't mean to be rude, but a stolen dragon was a bit more important than any wedding.

She said that was my opinion and I was welcome to it.

Emily won't help either. All she cares about is her stupid bridesmaid dress.

And Gordon has driven to the cash and carry to pick up all the drinks.

Mr McDougall is busy too, mending a hole in the roof of the church hall. He doesn't want any drips if it rains on his nephew's big day.

I'm going to go out now and search for more clues.

Eddie

From: Morton Pickle

To: Edward Smith-Pickle

Date: Tuesday 5 April

Subject: Re: Still missing

📎 **Attachments:** Sub

Dear Eddie

I was very shocked to get your messages. At the same time, I have to confess, I wasn't entirely surprised. The dragons are rare and extraordinary creatures, and I have often worried that some unscrupulous thief might try to snatch them.

You really shouldn't feel guilty. The whole operation sounds very professional, and I'm just glad they didn't hurt you while they were stealing Ziggy.

We have been fitting out my new submarine with equipment that we shall need if we're going to find the Kraken. We have spent a fortune on the latest sonar detectors and underwater cameras.

We had been planning to stay another night, but instead we shall set sail immediately, and search for the vile villain who has taken my dragon.

Please reassure your mother that I haven't forgotten her wedding. Of course I am going to give her away. I have even written my speech.

I shall see you very soon.

With love from

your affectionate uncle

Morton

From: Edward Smith-Pickle

To: Morton Pickle

Date: Wednesday 6 April

Subject: More bad news

 Attachments: The thief

Dear Uncle Morton

I have some more bad news.

Arthur has been stolen too.

This time I saw everything. I even know who took him.

I don't know the thief's name. Or where he went. But I do know what he looks like.

It happened this afternoon. Mr and Mrs McDougall came to tea. Mum and Gordon were talking to them about starters and puddings and candles and napkins and all the other wedding arrangements.

While they were talking, I went detecting with Arthur.

I found some interesting footprints on the beach.

I was studying them through the magnifying glass when I heard a loud bang.

I turned round and saw a man pointing a dart gun at Arthur.

There was another bang. This time the shooter didn't miss. Arthur fell out of the sky and landed on the sand with a splat.

A dart was sticking out of his tummy.

I ran towards him, but I wasn't quick enough. Before I got there, the thief had scooped Arthur up and waded out to his boat.

I screamed at him to stop, but he took no notice. He just sailed away across the sea.

I feel so stupid. It's all my fault. If I hadn't been looking at those footprints through your magnifying glass, I would have been guarding Arthur more carefully, and the thief wouldn't have got him.

I'm very sorry, Uncle Morton. I'm a terrible detective. I'm also the worst dragonsitter in the world.

Eddie

From: Edward Smith-Pickle

To: Morton Pickle

Date: Wednesday 6 April

Subject: Clueless

Attachments: Gordon's boat

Dear Uncle Morton

I have been detecting all day, but I haven't found any sign of your dragons.

First I searched the entire beach with your magnifying glass, but it was high tide and the sea had washed away any clues.

Then Gordon gave me a lift to the mainland.

He said he'd only help me if I wore a kilt at the wedding, but he was joking. At least I hope he was.

He dropped me off at the General Stores. Unfortunately they haven't seen any dragons recently.

I looked all round Lower Bisket, but I couldn't find any sign of Ziggy or Arthur.

Now we're back at your house, and it's dark, and I don't know what to do.

Eddie

From: Edward Smith-Pickle

To: Morton Pickle

Date: Thursday 7 April

Subject: The thief

Attachments: West Highland Gazette

Dear Uncle Morton

I have found the thief!

This afternoon we went to see the vicar. Mum and Gordon talked to him about hymns and prayers and rings and kissing and who signs the register and all the other details for Saturday.

Emily and I were getting a bit bored of talking about the wedding, so we did some painting instead.

The vicar didn't want us to get paint on his nice clean tablecloth, so he put out some newspaper, and that was where I saw the thief.

There was a picture of him in the paper.

I recognised him at once.

His name is Terry Crumpet. He has a castle near here.

I'm going to go there first thing tomorrow morning and take the dragons back.

Love from

Eddie

THE WEST HIGHLAND GAZETTE   6th April

New Dungeons Open at Crumpet Castle

A new exhibition has opened in the dungeons of Crumpet Castle. "You won't believe your eyes," promises Terry Crumpet, the castle's owner.

When Mr Crumpet bought the castle five years ago, he changed its name, and opened it to the public. He and his wife Gloriana opened a tearoom and a gift shop, and promised a wealth of excitements for all ages.

Visitor numbers have been low, but Mr Crumpet assures us that this is going to change. With the opening of the dungeons, he and Gloriana are confident of attracting thousands of tourists from home and abroad.

Although Mr Crumpet would not give us precise details of the new exhibits at Crumpet Castle, he did promise that visitors will not leave disappointed.

"We've got some amazing surprises down there," Mr Crumpet said. "Crumpet Castle is now the most exciting tourist experience for miles around. Bring your whole family for a fabulous day out."

From: Morton Pickle
To: Edward Smith–Pickle
Date: Thursday 7 April
Subject: Re: The thief

Dear Eddie

Many congratulations on your excellent detective work. I am very impressed that you managed to track down the thief so quickly.

I have never met Terry Crumpet, but I have heard of him. I must warn you, however, that nothing I have heard has been particularly good. There is little love for him in the village of Lower Bisket. He bought a beautiful castle, and not only changed its name to his own, but painted it bright pink, transforming a local landmark into an appalling eyesore.

Our preparations are almost complete. We are just testing the periscope before setting sail. I shall see you in time for elevenses.

And then we can confront Mr Crumpet together.

With love from

your affectionate uncle

Morton

Dear Uncle Morton

I've been waiting all morning, but there's no sign of your submarine.

If you don't get here soon, I'll have to go to Crumpet Castle without you.

Eddie

Dear Uncle Morton

I can't wait any longer. I'm going to Crumpet Castle on my own.

I wanted Mr McDougall to come with me, but he's not answering his phone. I think he must be practising his bagpipes for the big day.

I can't ask Gordon either, because he's gone to the airport to collect Granny.

Mum and Emily are icing the cake. I'm going to sneak out of the house and borrow your boat. If I'm quick, I'll be back with the dragons before they even notice I've gone.

If you get this, please meet me at Crumpet Castle.

Eddie

From: Edward Smith-Pickle

To: Morton Pickle

Date: Friday 8 April

Subject: Dungeons

 Attachments: Crumpet Castle; Prison

Dear Uncle Morton

I have found your dragons.

They're hungry and miserable, but at least they're still alive.

They are locked in the dungeons of Crumpet Castle.

I rowed all the way there. By the time I arrived, my arms were exhausted. I moored your boat at the jetty, and walked up to the castle.

The sun was shining and the walls looked extremely pink.

In the gatehouse was a man who said entry is strictly by ticket only and I would have to pay £4.

That was when I remembered the ticket which said ADMIT ONE.

Unfortunately it was on my bedside table.

I didn't want to go straight home. So I walked round the castle, searching for clues.

At the back was a dark hole covered by some metal bars. I knelt down and looked through.

There were the dragons!

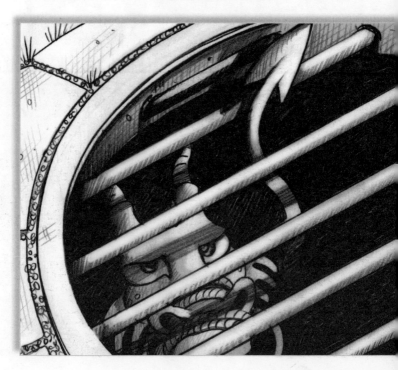

When Ziggy and Arthur saw me, they went wild. I had to tell them to shush. I didn't want Terry Crumpet to hear the noise.

He has wrapped their snouts in ropes, so they can't open their mouths wide enough to breathe fire.

Also he hasn't been feeding them properly. They're very thin. And extremely depressed.

I promised the dragons I'd be back ASAP.

When I walked away, I could hear them calling after me. The noise was awful. It sounded even worse than Mr McDougall's bagpipes.

I'm going to row to Crumpet Castle first thing tomorrow morning. If I'm quick, I'll be able to rescue the dragons and get back in time for Mum's wedding.

I left a message for Mr McDougall, asking him to give me a lift in his speedboat, but he hasn't called back.

He's probably in the pub with Gordon. They're having a night out with the lads.

I had asked Mum if I could go too, but she said I wasn't old enough to be one of the lads.

Could you give me a lift in your submarine instead?

Eddie

From: Edward Smith-Pickle

To: Morton Pickle

Date: Saturday 9 April

Subject: Rescued

Attachments: Inferno; Crumpets; Sherry

Dear Uncle Morton

I have some good news and some bad news.

The good news is your dragons are back.

The bad news is we're an hour late for Mum's wedding. I hope the vicar hasn't gone home.

This morning I crept out of your house. Mum and Emily were so busy with their hair that they didn't even notice me leaving.

I took the ticket and found some tools to free the dragons. Then I untied your boat from the jetty and rowed to Crumpet Castle.

I was the first visitor. The guard on the gate took my ticket and gave me a leaflet with a map. I followed the directions to the dungeons.

The dragons' door was locked with a padlock. Your bolt cutters snipped through that in two seconds. Your scissors cut the ropes almost as fast.

The three of us tiptoed up the stairs. I thought we'd escaped without being noticed, but I was wrong. When we got to the top, there were Terry Crumpet and his wife, blocking our way.

They stared at us.

We stared back.

I didn't know what to do.

Luckily Ziggy did. She breathed a great gust of fire in their direction.

Terry Crumpet threw himself one way. His wife went the other.

Their clothes were smoking and most of their hair was burnt off, but even so they picked themselves up and charged straight at us.

Ziggy breathed more fire at them.

Then she started flapping her wings.
Arthur and I jumped on her back.

Mr Crumpet grabbed her tail, and Mrs
Crumpet clung to the tip of one wing, but
they couldn't stop her.

Ziggy shook them off and flew into the air.

When I looked down, I could see the Crumpets jumping up and down, and waving their fists.

I waved back.

I'm very sorry, Uncle Morton. I left your boat behind. It's still tied up to the castle's jetty.

But at least Ziggy and Arthur are safely back at home.

I've never seen them so happy.

The only person who wasn't was Mum.

Apparently she's been worried sick.

She wouldn't go to the wedding without me, so she's been marching round the island in her wellies, searching every cliff and cave in case I'd been stranded.

Granny says it's the most stressful day of her life. I don't know how it can be.

She's just lying on the sofa with a bottle of sherry. But she says that's how she deals with stress.

Mum and Emily are changing into their dresses. Then Mr McDougall will pick us up in his speedboat and deliver us to the church.

I've just realised. We don't need a boat!

I'm going to go and tell Mum.

Eddie

From: Edward Smith–Pickle

To: Morton Pickle

Date: Sunday 10 April

Subject: Confetti

 Attachments: Taxi; Taxi 2; Confetti; Speech; Snooze; Dancing

Dear Uncle Morton

You missed a great wedding.

Everyone had to wait ages for us, but the vicar said it didn't matter. Apparently it's traditional for the bride to be late.

It can't be so traditional for her to arrive on the back of a dragon, but no one seemed to mind.

Mum had already called Mr McDougall and asked him to collect us in his boat.

I called him back and told him not to bother, because we didn't need a boat.

Mum said, "So how are we getting to the church?"

I said, "Your carriage awaits."

There was Ziggy, bending her neck and offering her back as if she'd spent her whole life giving people lifts.

Mum was a bit nervous, but she didn't
need much persuasion. She knew how late
we were.

She got on first, draping her dress over
Ziggy's back.

Granny went next. Then Emily. Then me.
Finally Arthur hopped aboard.

Once we were all sitting comfortably, Ziggy flapped her wings and we flew into the air.

It can't have been easy for her. She's not used to carrying so many people. But she still went really fast.

We swooped across the water from your island to the mainland.

There was one moment when Ziggy tipped right over and I thought we were all going to fall into the sea. But we didn't. And she landed us safely in the churchyard.

Luckily no one had gone home.

The wedding was very nice.

Mum looked amazing in her dress. So did Gordon in his kilt.

Because you weren't here, I had to give Mum away.

The vicar said it wasn't exactly conventional, but the Pickles have never been the most conventional family in the world.

Mr McDougall played his bagpipes. We all threw confetti. Granny couldn't stop crying, but she said they were tears of joy.

The party was very nice too. We had smoked salmon followed by venison and roast potatoes followed by chocolate mousse.

The speeches went on for hours, so it's probably a good thing you weren't here to give yours too.

Gordon's was the best. He told some jokes. Then he said Mum had made him the happiest man on the planet.

Granny cried again.

Emily did too, but that was because Mum said she couldn't have another chocolate mousse.

Gordon talked about you in his speech. He said he wanted to say thank you for introducing him and Mum.

Gordon talked about me and Emily too. He said he'll never replace our dad, but he's going to try and be a good stepfather to us.

Emily said a good stepfather would let her have another chocolate mousse.

Gordon said maybe for breakfast.

Your dragons behaved themselves very well.

Ziggy spent the whole time asleep on the grass in the churchyard. She must have been exhausted from all that flying.

Arthur took a big bite out of the cake, but we removed that layer, and it all looked fine.

The dancing went on till the middle of the night.

It was the best wedding ever.

I told Mum that, and she said she thought so too.

Now we're back on your island with Granny. Mum and Gordon stayed the night in the Lower Bisket Guesthouse. If you want to see them, they'll be coming here later to collect their bags and say goodbye before going on their honeymoon.

Love from

Eddie

From: Morton Pickle
To: Edward Smith-Pickle
Date: Sunday 10 April
Subject: Re: Confetti
Attachments: Propeller problem

Dear Eddie

I am so pleased to hear that you and the dragons are safe and well. Congratulations on defeating the Crumpets.

I'm terribly sorry that I missed your mother's wedding. Shortly after we left port, the second propeller failed, and my first mate insisted on turning back.

You'll be glad to hear that the propeller has been mended, and we are intending to leave imminently. If we make good progress around the coast, we should reach my island shortly after nightfall.

Come down to the jetty and find us first thing tomorrow morning. I am looking forward to welcoming you, Emily and my mother aboard, and serving you a slap-up breakfast in the mess.

With love from

your affectionate uncle

Morton

From: Edward Smith–Pickle

To: Morton Pickle

Date: Monday 11 April

Subject: Help!

📎 **Attachments:** Hush; Crumpet

Dear Uncle Morton

Terry Crumpet is here on your island!

I've just seen him.

He saw me too. In fact, he chased me up the hill and back to your house.

I had gone down to the jetty to meet you. But when I got there, I couldn't see any sign of a submarine. Instead I saw Mr Crumpet's speedboat tied to the jetty.

I was just about to go and have a closer look when I heard a loud bang and felt a dart whoosh past my cheek.

I turned round and there was Terry Crumpet, pointing his dart gun straight at my chest.

54

"You stole my beasts," he said. "I want them back."

I said they weren't his in the first place, but he just laughed.

"Finders keepers," he said. Then he shot at me again. Luckily I dodged out of the way just in time.

I ran back home as fast as I could. Now I'm hiding inside your house with Granny and Emily and the dragons.

Terry Crumpet is pacing round your garden with his gun.

We don't know what to do.

I've tried calling the police and Mr McDougall, but the phone doesn't seem to be working.

I know you probably won't get this in time. But if you do, please come and help!

Eddie

From: Edward Smith-Pickle

To: Morton Pickle

Date: Monday 11 April

Subject: Justice

Attachments: Knock-out; Pick-up; Drop-off

Dear Uncle Morton

You don't have to worry about Terry Crumpet. He's not going to be coming back here again.

The dragons just chased him off your island.

It was his own fault. He shouldn't have broken your window.

He did it with the end of his gun. I suppose he was planning to climb through and grab the dragons.

But Arthur flew through the hole first and attacked him.

Terry Crumpet ducked out of the way.

Arthur whirled round and came back for a second attempt.

Terry Crumpet lifted his dart gun in the air. He was aiming at Arthur, trying to get a good shot.

I ran out of the front door and screamed at him to stop, but he took no notice.

Luckily Ziggy came too. She flew straight at Terry Crumpet and knocked him over with one great swipe of her tail.

Terry Crumpet rolled over on the grass. Then he pointed his gun at Ziggy.

Before he could shoot, she breathed a fire–ball in his direction.

His gun melted like ice cream.

Terry Crumpet jumped to his feet and ran.

But he wasn't fast enough.

Ziggy flew after him.

When she opened her mouth, I thought she was going to burn him alive.

Instead she bit him on the bum.

Terry Crumpet screamed and struggled, but Ziggy wouldn't let go.

She clamped her jaws around his bottom. Then she flapped her wings and flew into the air.

He was hanging from her mouth, waving his arms and shouting.

He said some terrible words. I had to put my hands over Emily's ears.

Ziggy didn't care. She just flew higher and higher, carrying Terry Crumpet in her jaws.

Out of the garden. Over the beach. Out to sea.

"Let me go!" Terry Crumpet yelled. "You stupid beast! You dumb monster! Let me go!"

So she did.

Terry Crumpet fell through the air like a stone.

He landed in the sea with a huge splash.

He didn't drown. In fact he's fine. His speedboat came and picked him up.

I watched through the binoculars. I could see his wife pulling him aboard.

She gave him a towel. Then they sped away across the sea in the direction of Crumpet Castle.

I don't think Mr and Mrs Crumpet will ever try to steal another dragon.

Love from

Eddie

From: Morton Pickle
To: Edward Smith-Pickle
Date: Tuesday 12 April
Subject: Re: Justice

Dear Eddie

Congratulations on dealing with Terry Crumpet. He is clearly a nasty piece of work. As soon as I get home, I shall report him to the Royal Society for the Prevention of Cruelty to Animals.

The submarine suffered a couple of last-minute hitches, but we'll be setting off in the next few minutes. I shall be home by teatime at the latest.

See you at the jetty.

With love from

your affectionate uncle

Morton

From: Edward Smith-Pickle
To: Morton Pickle
Date: Wednesday 13 April
Subject: Barbie
Attachments: BBQ

Dear Uncle Morton

We are having a barbecue for tea, and you're invited.

Mr McDougall is helping us. This afternoon we gathered lots of driftwood on the beach. Now he and Granny are building a bonfire near the jetty.

Granny bought thirty-six sausages and eight chicken legs, so there should be enough for the dragons and us and you and all your crew too.

I've got my binoculars. I'll be watching out for your submarine.

Love from

Eddie

From: Morton Pickle

To: Edward Smith-Pickle

Date: Wednesday 13 April

Subject: Re: Barbie

📎 **Attachments:** The Atlantic Ocean

Dear Eddie

I'm terribly sorry to have missed your barbecue.

We got a report that the Kraken had been spotted half way between Norway and the Shetland Islands, and had to head in that direction immediately.

Our sonar has just spotted some interesting activity.

Full speed ahead!

M

The Dragonsitter's Island

Josh Lacey
Illustrated by Garry Parsons

Dear Uncle Morton,
The McDougalls are here. Mr McDougall won't stop
shouting and waving his arms. He has lost three sheep
in a week. Now he wants to take your dragons away
and lock them in his barn till the police arrive.

Eddie is dragonsitting on Uncle Morton's Scottish
island. But something is eating the local sheep.
Can Eddie find the real culprit?

Praise for *The Dragonsitter*:
'Ideal for young readers,
and belly-busting laughter
for all the family'
We Love This Book

9781783440450 £4.99

The Dragonsitter's Party

Josh Lacey

Illustrated by Garry Parsons

Dear Uncle Morton

Can you come to my birthday party? It's going to be great.
We're having a magician. Mum says your dragons aren't
invited, but you can take some cake home for them.

It's Eddie's birthday and he's looking forward to a birthday
party filled with fun, games and . . . dragons?
Ziggy and Arthur are the unexpected guests, but their
idea of a good time involves eating everything in sight
and ruining the party magician's tricks.
Is Eddie in for the wrong kind of
birthday surprise?

Praise for *The Dragonsitter*:
'Josh Lacey's comic timing
is impeccable'
Books for Keeps

9781783442294   £4.99

The Dragonsitter
to the
Rescue

Josh Lacey
Illustrated by Garry Parsons

Dear Uncle Morton
I have to tell you some bad news. We have lost one of
your dragons. He's somewhere in London, but I don't
know where.

Sightseeing is the last thing on Eddie's mind when the
dragons escape on a trip to London. Will he find them
before they get into hot water?

9781783443291   £4.99